I0726542

Dodo

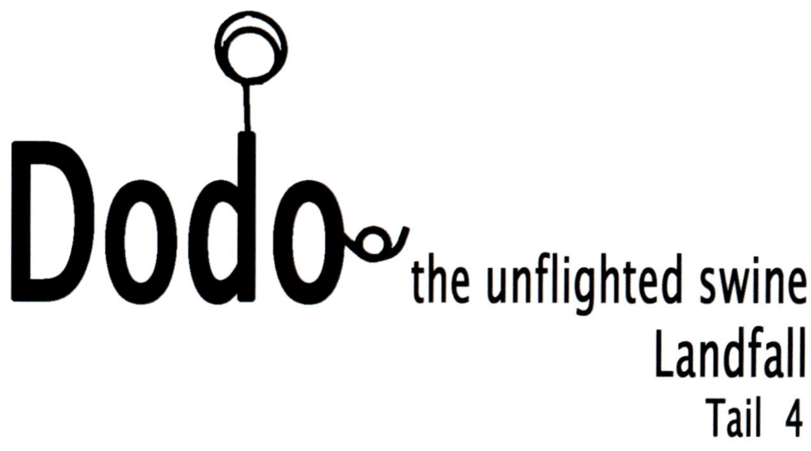

the unflighted swine
Landfall
Tail 4

Tale & Imagery
Terry & Boyd Krueger

Puzzledmemorys ~ Presses
KRUEGERPHOTOGRAPHY DIGITALDESIGN
©2018

This publication contains the opinions and ideas of its author. It is intended to provide helpful and informative material on the subjects addressed in the publication. The author and publisher specifically disclaim all responsibility for any liability, loss or risk, personal or otherwise, which is incurred as a consequence, directly or indirectly, of the use and application of any of the contents of this book.

WORKBOOK PRESS LLC
187 E Warm Springs Rd,
Suite B285, Las Vegas, NV 89119, USA

Website: https://workbookpress.com/
Hotline: 1-888-818-4856
Email: admin@workbookpress.com

Ordering Information:
Quantity sales. Special discounts are available on quantity purchases by corporations, associations, and others. For details, contact the publisher at the address above.

Library of Congress Control Number:
ISBN-13:   978-1-961845-63-3 (Paperback Version)
             978-1-961845-80-0 (Digital Version)

REV. DATE: 07.12.2023

For Deborah, thank you for introducing a pearl.

Dodo◦ had been lost on a raft of seaweed in the ocean for an unknown length of time.

He was now lost on the shore.

Where was he ?

Dodo had found and followed footprints after being washed ashore, but they seemed to lead nowhere.

He found another set of strange footprints.
He followed them, but found no one.

He was hungry but things which looked like food
tasted like the seaweed he had been eating while adrift in the ocean.

All of the water was saltwater... he was thirsty, hungry and lost.

Dodo saw something in the sand... Could it be food ?

No... it was just a sand dollar !

Dodo was lost. He needed a plan.

He found a seaweed-covered ledge on a rock and climbed up.
He snuggled down into the seaweed to plan and fell asleep.

Dodo awoke, looked around and
he could hardly believe what he saw.

A beautiful pig, standing on the sand and gazing out to the ocean.

The beautiful pig turned slightly and Dodo could only stare...

this beautiful pig was just like him...

another pig with a strange appendage protruding straight
up from her back, a weird wing with an odd twist
at the tip.

Dodo wondered whether he should introduce himself.

Would this stunning pig, so much like him, yet so different,
want to meet him ? She was beautiful, her skin shimmered
in the light and pearls hung on her body.

He was matte gray.

As he stared at her, this beautiful pig saw him
and started walking towards him.

"Hello, my name is Pearl E Pig."
Dodo replied, "I'm Dodo Swine."

In unison, they both said, "I have never met another with a strange
appendage protruding straight up from their back, a weird wing
with an odd twist at the tip."

Dodo and Pearl talked about their adventures, their families and
their lives and dreams for the future.

They both had tried to find wings...
Dodo at the wing stores,

Pearl at a butterfly sanctuary.

Each described the wings of their dreams.

12

Alas, neither of them had found wings nor the ability to fly.

Their lives were to be unflighted, with
strange appendages protruding straight up from their backs,
weird wings with odd twists at the tip.

Dodo confided in Pearl that he had been on his way to meet bison
in Montana, when he was dropped off at a beach, Montaña de Oro.
There were no bison and he was not in the state of Montana.
And as he wandered the shoreline wondering what to do,
a rogue wave had washed him out into the Pacific Ocean.

Pearl listened in awe to Dodo's tale.

When he finished, Pearl informed him that he had been
washed up on the gulf coast of Alabama.

Dodo was speechless. He had been on the coast of California
and now he was on the gulf coast of Alabama. How could it be
that he had drifted that far and survived ?

Dodo awoke with a jolt... he was confused...
He crawled up on the rock to have a look around.

... he was on the same shore he had been washed up on...
no beautiful Pearl E Pig in sight... he was all alone, again.

Pearl E Pig had been a dream.

He was lost and alone.
As Dodo stared out over the intertidal, he thought he saw someone.
Would she be willing to help a swine with such a sad tale ?
Was she even real ?

Dodo crawled down off of the rock and

headed towards her.

Dodo~ was gathered up by the woman. She was real.

She took him to eat real food

and to get a shower.

Dodo˚ was given a clean, comfortable bed
where he promptly fell fast asleep.

He was well-fed, clean, warm and safe.

Dodo dreamt of seaweed and Pearl E Pig... and future adventures.

www.ingramcontent.com/pod-product-compliance
Lightning Source LLC
Chambersburg PA
CBRC090352200726
48295CB00021B/132